NOSE DROPS

Dear Samantha —
Stop + smell the roses!

Larry Shles

by Larry Shles

Dedicated to my father who,
wittingly or unwittingly
depending upon one's sense of humor,
passed down the word play genes.

A special thanks to
Diana who helped bend my nose back into joint,
Carolyn who pointed it in the right direction,
and Linda who provided valuable technical assistance.

Other books written and illustrated by Larry Shles

Moths and Mothers, Feathers and Fathers
Hoots and Toots and Hairy Brutes
Hugs and Shrugs
Aliens In My Nest
Do I Have To Go To School Today?
Scooter's Tail Of Terror

Books illustrated by Larry Shles

Flamingo Knees
The Knees Knock Again

NOSE DROPS

by Larry Shles
Squib Publications 1994

Geoffrey dropped into this story from out of nowhere.

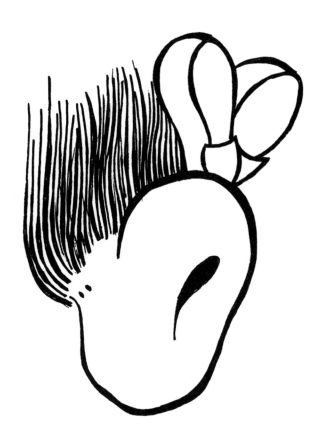

"How did I get into this *book*?!" he wondered with alarm. "I've been removed from my face. I am just a *nose*!"

Geoffrey looked around. He was the only character in sight. When he saw his name printed on the page, he really panicked.

"This story is about *me*!" he exclaimed. "I don't belong here. I have page fright. I have to find a way out of this book and back to my face."

He searched
high.

He searched
low.

He even searched

between the lines.

There was no escape.

Geoffrey couldn't bear the thought of being a character in this book. After all, nothing interesting ever happened to him. His story would be boring. And besides, he was just a nose.

What if he developed a pimple?! When you are just a nose and you have a pimple, there is *nowhere* else for a person to stare!

"Geoffrey, Geoffrey," a voice called faintly in the distance.

"Thank goodness," he sighed. "I am saved. My face must have discovered that I am missing. It sounds like it is calling to me from the end of this story."

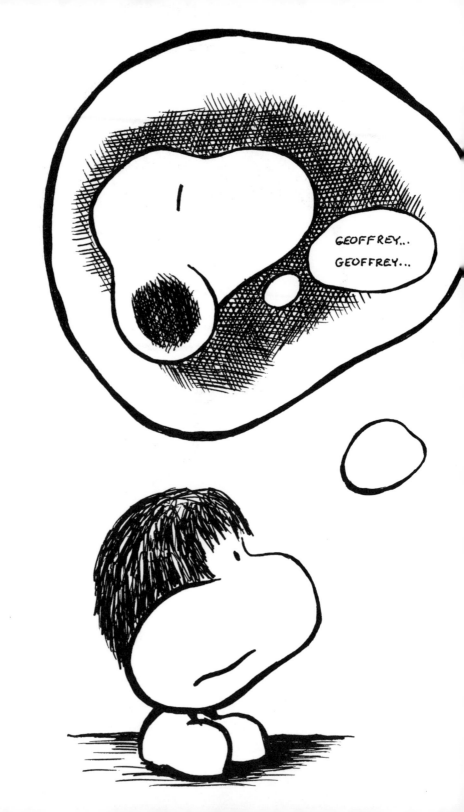

Since Geoffrey had never seen the face to which he belonged, he had no idea who was calling to him. His imagination ran wild.

GEOFFREY...
GEOFFREY...

If he could somehow find his way to the last page, he would be reunited with his face. Geoffrey developed a plan. He would search for a shortcut to the end of the book. To help protect himself from danger, he donned a disguise and became Geoffrey, Private Nose.

Cautiously, he proceeded to the next page....

....and found himself in a dingy nose dive.

"Excuse me," he announced. "I seem to have misplaced my face. I think it is at the end of the book waiting for me. Is there a shortcut to the last page?"

The notorious pirate, Peg Nose Pete, piped up.

"First, kid, dump the disguise! You're not fooling anyone. Second, that is not your face calling to you. Forget about finding your face. Stay with us and be the main character in our story. You won't believe the adventures that await you."

"I have a word of warning for you, though. Do not look for a shortcut to the end of your story. And whatever you do, *do not sneak a peek at the last page of this book*!"

"Peg Nose, I don't understand," said Geoffrey. "How can I be a character in this book? I am just a *nose*."

"You wouldn't be the first beak to make it big in books," Peg Nose answered. "Come with me to the next page. You will begin to understand."

"Wow!" Geoffrey shouted. "That's the famous Roman nose, Julius Sneezer!"

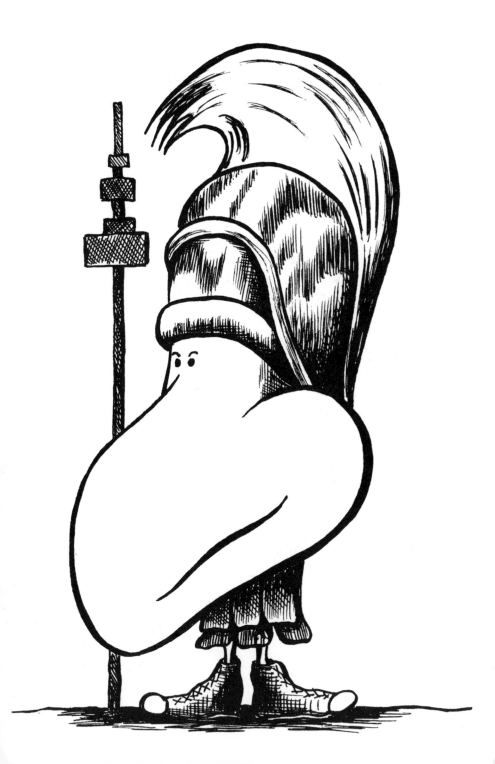

"And there is Noses receiving a new commandment!"

"I don't believe it! That is Dr. Hypotenose. He is a great genius."

"You know all the right angles, Doctor," said Geoffrey. "Should I stop searching for my face and become a character in this book?"

"Absolutely!" said Dr. Hypotenose. "You can become a powerful educational tool. Your stories will teach valuable lessons and essential skills to children."

"Let me give you one piece of advice, though. Do not skip any pages. *And under no circumstances should you sneak a peek at the last page of this book.* Now this is my plan for you...."

Look, Pete, look.
See Geoffrey run.

Run, Geoffrey, run.

THE RUNNY NOSE

Run, run,

run.

"Then you will introduce your new readers to the classic fables. In one of these stories you will be His Royal Sinus, Olde King Colde. In this updated version, your subjects seek ways to unblock those royal passageways."

"In another fable you will race the tortoise and the nose hare. You will teach children about values, such as the importance of hard work, persistence and patience. You will become a wonderful role model."

"This is going to be great fun!" Geoffrey said. "I have decided to stay in your book. I can't wait to see what happens to me next!"

THE TWEAKLY READER
BOOK CONTEST WINNER:
KIDS PICK
GEOFFREY

SOON TO BE PUBLISHED: GEOFFREY SPEAKS OUT
AGAINST PEER PRESSURE, DRUGS, VIOLENCE AND THE
DAILY USE OF NASAL SPRAYS IN "JUST SAY NOSE!"

"You have made a wise decision," said Dr. Hypotenose. "Your books are destined to win major literary awards. There will be educational activities, teacher's manuals, games, workbooks...."

"Books, Schmooks!" Twitch Scratchmore exclaimed with a sneer. "I overheard the Doctor's plans for you, Geoffrey. Don't listen to his advice. If you hire *me* as your manager, I will make you rich and famous. Here is my plan. We will begin by making a few minor changes..."

"First you will need a nose job. You are quite a honker. Then we will have to give you a snappier name like Pokey or Sniffy. Also, there is no future for you in books. People aren't reading much anymore. The big bucks are in television. You will have your own prime-time show."

SPIDER SNOOT

"Each week you will portray a different action hero. This will help create the macho-nose image necessary for your success."

"Once your show wins its time slot, you'll be ready for the big screen," Twitch proclaimed. "The public loves action and gore. Your first role will be that of Jack the Dripper. This crazed fiend refuses to cover himself when he sneezes and spreads a plague throughout London."

"High-tech makeup will transform you into 'Tyranno-Snorus, The Lizard of Schnoz' in your second feature."

"Finally you will become a romantic
lead playing opposite Dripsy Nose Lee. This
steamy love story unblocks every sinus in
the audience. It will be a four hanky movie!"

"You will be on your way, Geoffrey!
Imagine it....."

COMING SOON
GEOFFREY
IN

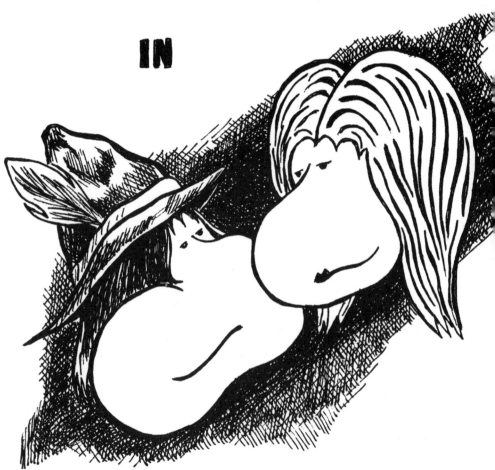

NOSE ENCOUNTERS
OF THE ABSURD KIND

"....magazine features...."

"....sneaker endorsements...."

"....and an adorable Geoffrey doll that children will want to cuddle and take to bed."

"I can lift you to the top, Geoffrey!" exclaimed Twitch. "You must take your time, though. Don't skip any steps. *And under no circumstances should you sneak a peek......*"

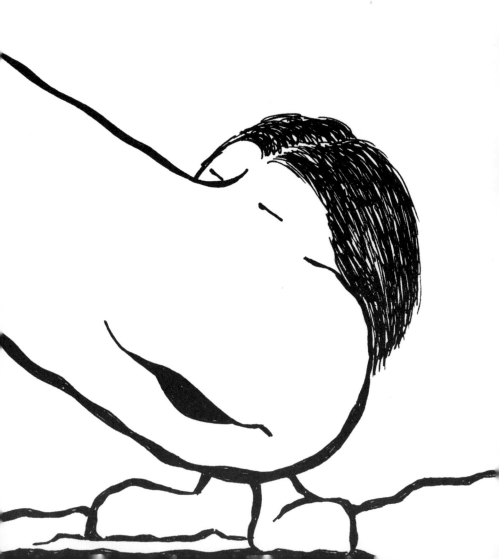

But the warning fell on a deaf nose. Geoffrey couldn't contain himself. He had to peek. He rushed past the next forty-five pages. He had to see himself in a hot red sports car and a mansion with a hot tub and.....

NOSE OU
THAT BO
TURN OU
LIGHT AN
TO SLEEP
INSTANT

"Uh, oh...."

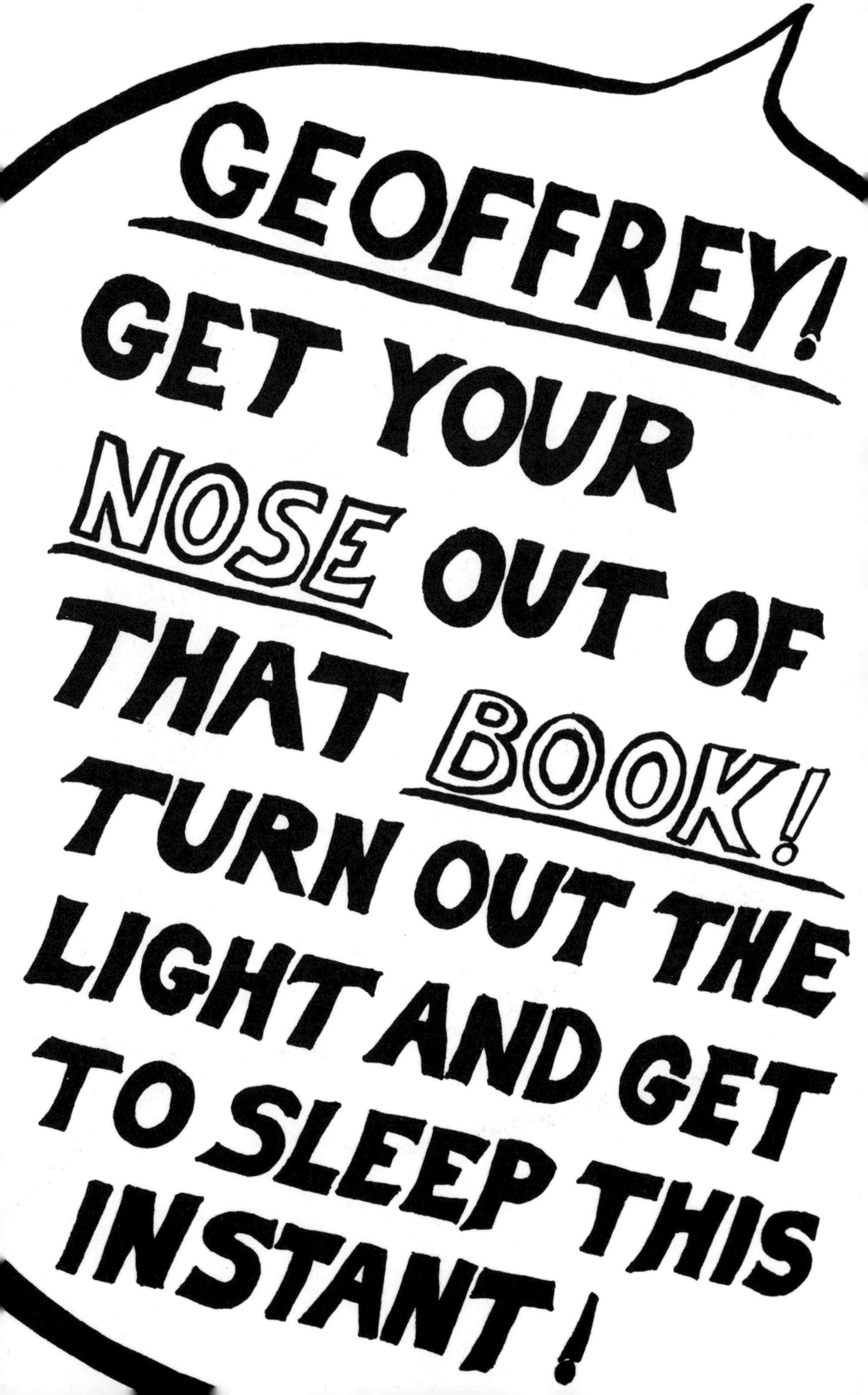
GEOFFREY! GET YOUR NOSE OUT OF THAT BOOK! TURN OUT THE LIGHT AND GET TO SLEEP THIS INSTANT!

INTRODUCING GEOFFREY IN

NOSE DROPS

NOSE D

In a wink, Geoffrey was yanked out of the book and returned to his rightful face.

"Oh, no," he sighed. "I don't want to be here. I belong back in my story. I want to be rich and famous."

Then his thoughts turned to Peg Nose and Twitch and Dr. Hypotenose. As if by magic, the whole gang appeared at the foot of his bed.

"I believe we *did* warn you not to peek," chided Twitch.

Geoffrey couldn't help giggling. He felt richer already with these wonderful new friends in his life.

"Wait for me, guys," Geoffrey said. "I'll visit you the next time I drop into your book. You will always be a part of me."

Then Geoffrey saw a new book waiting for him on the night stand. He couldn't wait until morning. He plunged in.